The Lil' Bulldog, Tridz Farm Summer Camp.
By Felice Herrig.

Illustrated by Kirk Herrig.

For information regarding permission, write to:

Sevenhorns Publishing
Attention: Permissions
276 5th Avenue, Suite 704
New York, New York 10001

Published by www.sevenhornspublishing.com

Design: Branded Human

Library of Congress Control Number: 2021937974

ISBN: 978-1-7363887-6-1 (hardcover)
        978-1-7363887-7-8 (pbk.)
        978-1-7363887-8-5 (ebook)

Printed in the U.S.A.

www.sevenhornspublishing.com

THE LIL' BULLDOG

Tridz Farm Summer Camp

by Felice Herrig

Illustrated by Kirk Herrig

SEVEN HORNS PUBLISHING

www.sevenhornspublishing.com

The Lil' Bulldog and Friends

The Lil' Bulldog (LBD)

Quinn the Cat

Shawnee the Mouse

Sock'em the Sock Monkey

Simon the Salamander

Ethereal the Bunny

P. U. Stanky the Skunk

Toober the Mole

Kozzi & The Mouse

Gigi the Otter

Shannon the Pink Bird

Worm & Chocolate Bunny

Billy Jo Bob

Fifi Jo Bob

Bobby Jo Bob

Beauford Jo Bob

Willie Jo Bob

Grandpa Tridz

Socks and shoes, toothbrushes and shampoos...

And let's not forget their beloved sock monkey, Sock 'em!

"Bags are packed, new adventures await," said The Lil' Bulldog. "No time to waste, we mustn't be late!"

Full of excitement, The Lil' Bulldog, Quinn the Cat, Shawnee the Mouse, and Sock 'em the Sock Monkey get on the road, eager to make new memories together, down on the farm at Tridz Farm Summer Camp.

When The Lil' Bulldog and friends arrive down on the farm, they are greeted by their camp guide, P.U. Stanky.

"Hello Campers! You're in for a busy summer!" said P.U. Stanky.
"But for now, it's time to meet the Tridz!"

"Welcome campers!" said Grandpa Tridz. "We are the Tridz family, and this is our farm. Here, we do a little bit of work and have a little bit of fun, all rolled into one!"

"Banquet Night is the first night of summer camp at Tridz Farm," said Grandpa Tridz. "There's lots of food, laughter, and chitter-chatter."

The Lil' Bulldog can't get enough of the rainbow cupcakes with buttercream frosting.

Quinn the Cat slurps and glurps chocolate milk, while Kozzi gazes at her in awe. It looks like she has a new admirer!

And Shawnee the Mouse is happily feasting on 52 kinds of cheese.

Sock 'em would rather play with his food than eat it.

Full and tired from the night before, in the morning the campers plan on sleeping in.

NOPE!

"Wakey, wakey," said P.U. Stanky. "Let's go get some eggs and bakey."

"But it's so early," said The Lil' Bulldog.

"Yup, that's how we do things down on the farm," said P.U. Stanky. "How else would we get all our chores done in time for dinner?"

"Chores?" the campers ask, bewildered.

"Of course, chores!" says P. U. Stanky. "And germs, germs, germs, everywhere germs," he says, spraying their bags, one by one.

Help The Lil' Bulldog find:

Mouse   Worm   Chocolate Bunny

11

"Cows need to be milked everyday, rain or shine," said Fifi Jo Bob. "So grab a bucket, choose a cow, and take hold of an udder. It's time to make some butter!"

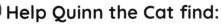

Help Quinn the Cat find:

Worm

Sock' em

Chocolate Bunny

Mimi the cow reminds The Lil' Bulldog to be gentle with her teats!

13

"Now that you've milked the cows, it's time to churn that butter," said Fifi Jo Bob. "Shake, shake, shake, and mix and stir."

"And let's not forget to turn and churn!" said Willie Jo Bob.

Sock'em would rather do gymnastics on the churn than make butter with it.

15

That night as a reward for a job well done, the happy campers were treated to movie night.

They drizzled the butter that they churned from the cows that they milked all over their popcorn.

And let's not forget to pass the salt.

Help Shawnee the Mouse find:

Worm   Another   Chocolate
        Worm   Bunny

Elderberry

Huckleberry

Goji berry

Quack-a-doodle-do!

No time to lose, no time to snooze. It's the beginning of a brand new day, and the campers woke up ready to explore.

The day began in the fields picking berries.

"Blackberries, and blueberries, raspberries, and strawberries," said Fifi Jo Bob. "DO you know how many different kinds of berries there are?"

Fun Facts:

Berries are good for brain health! They contain nutrients that boost learning and memory.

The scientific study of blackberries is called *batology*!

Gooseberry

Boysenberry

"10! ... 100! ... 1 million!"

Campers shouted out answers from all directions.

"Close," said Fifi. "There are over 400 different types of berries around the world. Some have strange names, like Goji and açaí."

"And let's not forget about the elderberries," said Grandpa Tridz. "Now that we've collected all our berries, it's time for us to make some pies!"

"I love pie!" shouted The Lil' Bulldog. "It's berry delicious!"

Fifi Jo Bob laughed. "I love me some pie, too!" she said. "Alright campers, you know what to do. It's time to mix and stir, mix and stir. And let's not forget to fold and turn!"

Help The Lil' Bulldog find:

Worm   Shannon the Pink Bird   Chocolate Bunny

That night as a reward for a job well done the campers were treated to a Game Night.

They topped off the pies they made from the berries they picked with scoops of ice cream.

Some ate cherry pie, while others ate blueberry pie.

Some even ate the Gooseberry pie.

And let's not forget about the mixed berry pie!

Help Quinn the Cat find:

Worm Mouse Chocolate Bunny

"Knock, knock, knock! It's 5 o' clock," said P.U. Stanky. "So roll up your sleeves! We're about to pick some corn, squash, and peas."

They started the day harvesting the fields.

And this day they had an especially big yield.

Help Shawnee the Mouse find:

Bug   The Mouse   Sock 'em the Sock Monkey

After picking vegetables in the fields, it was time to shuck some corn.

"Shucking and husking, husking and shucking. It's all the same, same, same," said Willie Jo Bob.

"Come on everyone, let's have some fun!" said Bobby Jo Bob. "I'm about to show you all just how it's done."

"Husk and shuck and shuck away," said Willie Jo Bob.

"And let's not forget to peel, peel, peel!" chimed in P.U. Stanky.

Help The Lil' Bulldog find:

Mouse Worm Chocolate
Bunny

That night, for a job well done they were rewarded with a campfire and scarecrow stories.

They used the vegetables that they picked to make shish kabobs and roasted the corn that they husked for corn on the cob.

The Tridz took turns telling spooky scarecrow stories to keep the campers spooked silly.

Help Quinn the Cat find:

Mouse   Worm   Bug

Quack-a-doodle-do!

"It's 5 a.m. again. Time to feed those chickens and gather some eggs," said P.U. Stanky. "Brown, green, and blue and rainbow, too. Try not to drop'em, or we'll have too few."

Fun Facts:

Not all snakes lay eggs! The Colombian red tail boa gives birth to live young.

There are only two mammals in the world that lay eggs! The platypus is one of them. Do you see the platypus?

A pysanka is a traditional Ukranian Easter egg that's decorated with Ukrainian folk art.

Help Shawnee the Mouse find:

Bug   Mouse   2 Flies

We've gathered all the eggs," The Lil' Bulldog says. "The Tridz hid needles in the haystacks for us to find," she tells her friends. "Let's hurry up and find 'em before it gets too dark!"

"I don't see any," says Shawnee the Mouse.

"Me either," sighs Quinn the Cat.

"Where could they be?" wonders Sock 'em the Sock Monkey.

"Hmmmm," says Simon the Salamander.

"Oops, we forgot to hide the needles," Willie Jo Bob says. "Oh, what a mess!"

"Let's not stress," says The Lil' Bulldog. "We should find a way to make use of all this hay."

"Yes, yes, yes!" P.U. Stanky says. "Let's clean this mess. Gather, gather, gather. Stick and stack, and stick and stack, until you've got a big ol' jumble bundle of hay."

Help The Lil' Bulldog find:

Bee   Fly   Chocolate Bunny

That night, for a job well done, they were rewarded with a fun-filled night of arts and crafts.

"Let's get out those jumble bundles and make some scarecrows," said P.U. Stanky.

"What are scarecrows?" asked Quinn the Cat.

"They're hay people," said Shawnee the Mouse.

"That's right," said The Lil' Bulldog. "They help protect the crops."

Help Quinn the Cat find:

Bug Mouse Worm

For breakfast on their last day at Tridz Farm, the campers ate omelettes made from the eggs they gathered the day before.

"I'm going to miss you guys," said Shawnee the Mouse.

"Me too," said Quinn the Cat.

"Me 3!" said Sock 'em the Sock Monkey.

"Me 100!" said Simon the Salamander.

"Me 1 million!" said Kozzi.

"Promise we'll text each other everyday," said The Lil' Bulldog.

"Bags are packed, and we're on our way," said P.U. Stanky. "It's time to go. Let's not delay!"

Help Shawnee the Mouse find:

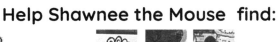

Fly   Worm   Mouse

"Remember, lil' ones, work hard, but not so hard you have no fun," said Grandpa Tridz. "And when the work is through, you'll be rewarded for a job well done."

"Thank you for all your help," said P.U. Stanky.

The Lil' Bulldog and friends thanked Grandpa Tridz and all the Tridz for teaching them to work hard and have tons of fun on the farm.

They said their goodbyes with hugs and lots of love.

Help The Lil' Bulldog find:

Mouse Worm Chocolate
Bunny

39

One more fun thing...

The Lil' Bulldog loves to see her initials everywhere! How many times can you spot the letters LBD hidden throughout the book?

Answer: 34

CPSIA information can be obtained
at www.ICGtesting.com
Printed in the USA
LVHW070117130921
697443LV00031B/459

9 781736 388761